Our Emotions and Behavior

Take a Deep Breath

Sue Graves

**Illustrated by
Desideria Guicciardini**

free spirit
PUBLISHING®

Niko and Ruby were going to school. Then Ruby saw Alex. He was taking Jet for a walk.

Ruby didn't like dogs. She said all dogs were **SCary.** She hid behind Mom.

Mom said that Jet was a nice dog.
She said he only wanted to be friends.
She told Ruby to **calm down** and to
take a deep breath.

2

Ruby took a deep breath.
She didn't hide behind Mom.

She even gave Jet a **little pat.**

At school, Andy had a swimming lesson. Miss Button said Andy had to jump into the water.

But Andy did not want to jump into the water. He did not like water going into his ears. He said it made a funny noise.

Miss Button told Andy to **take a deep breath** and to **think calm thoughts.**

8

Andy took a deep breath.
He jumped into the water.

Miss Button said Andy was
very brave.

Andy was so pleased, he jumped in again . . . and **again** . . . and **again!**

During recess at school, Dan cut his knee. He began to cry. Andy told him to calm down and to take a deep breath.

Dan took a **deep breath.**
He stopped crying.

Mr. Harris washed Dan's knee and put a bandage on his cut.

14

He gave Dan a sticker for
being brave.
Dan was pleased.

15

In the afternoon, the children put
on a play for the whole school.

But Josh did not want to go on the stage.
He did not want everyone looking at him.

Miss Button told Josh to **take a deep breath** and to **keep calm.**

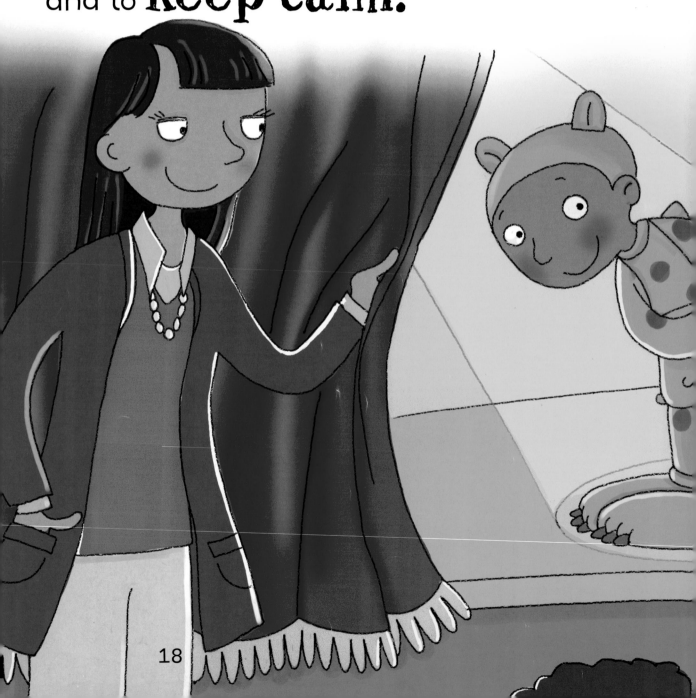

18

Josh took **a deep breath.**
He went on the stage. Everyone clapped
and cheered.

At story time, Miss Button got a book from the bookshelf. A spider landed on her arm. Miss Button did not like spiders.

"Take a deep breath!" said all the children.

Everyone laughed!

21

Can you tell the story of what happens when Jesse has a turn on the big slide?

How do you think Jesse felt before she went on the slide? How did she feel afterward?

A note about sharing this book

The **Our Emotions and Behavior** series has been developed to provide a starting point for further discussion about children's feelings and behavior, in relation both to themselves and to other people.

Take a Deep Breath
This story explores in a reassuring way how to overcome fears or nerves by taking a deep breath and staying calm.

The book aims to encourage children to have a developing awareness of their own needs, views, and feelings, and to be sensitive to the needs, views, and feelings of others.

Picture story
The picture story on pages 22 and 23 provides an opportunity for speaking and listening. Children are encouraged to tell the story illustrated in the panels: Jesse is scared of going on the big slide, but she also really wants to join her friends. She takes a deep breath and gives it a try. Jesse finds to her happy surprise that the slide is very fun.

How to use the book
The book is designed for adults to share with either an individual child or a group of children, and as a starting point for discussion.

The book also provides visual support and repeated words and phrases to build confidence in children who are starting to read on their own.

Before reading the story
Choose a time to read when you and the children are relaxed and have time to share the story.

Spend time looking at the illustrations and discussing what the book may be about before reading it together.

After reading, talk about the book with the children

- What was the story about? Have the children ever felt nervous or afraid? What were they afraid of? Were they able to get over their fear? If so, how? Talk about coping with and overcoming fears they still have. Who can they turn to for help when they feel afraid?

- Have any of the children been afraid of animals such as dogs or cats, or of insects such as spiders, wasps, or bees? Ask them to explore what seems to make some animals and insects scarier than others.

- Find out how many children are afraid of water and learning to swim. Point out that people differ in what scares them and that what frightens one person may not frighten another.

- Talk about the way the characters in the book used the strategy of taking a deep breath and keeping calm. Invite all the children to breathe in and then out slowly. Ask them how they feel after doing this. Point out that taking a deep breath can be very calming.

- Turn to the end of the story where Josh feels afraid and doesn't want to go on stage in front of everyone. Ask the children how Josh felt before his performance. How do they think he felt afterward? Ask the children if they have had similar experiences. Invite them to share their experiences.

- Look at the picture story. Ask the children to talk about Jesse's concerns about going on the big slide. How did she feel before she went on the slide? How did she feel afterward? Again, invite the children to share their experiences of similar occasions. Ask them to tell the others how they overcame their fears.

- Suggest that children draw "before" and "after" pictures of times when they have been scared or anxious in the past. In the "before" picture, have them draw themselves and what they were scared of. In the "after" picture, have them draw themselves staying calm and overcoming their anxieties.

Published in North America by Free Spirit Publishing Inc., Minneapolis, Minnesota, 2013.

Library of Congress Cataloging-in-Publication Data
Graves, Sue, 1950–
   Take a deep breath / Sue Graves ; illustrated by Desideria Guicciardini.
      pages cm. — (Our emotions and behavior)
   Audience: Age 4 to 8.
   ISBN-13: 978-1-57542-446-0
   ISBN-10: 1-57542-446-0
   1. Fear in children—Juvenile literature. I. Guicciardini, Desideria,
illustrator. II. Title.
   BF723.F4G727 2013
   152.4'6–dc23
                                             2013012339

Reading Level Grade 1; Interest Level Ages 4–8; Fountas & Pinnell Guided Reading Level I

10 9 8 7 6 5 4 3 2 1
Printed in China
S14100513

Free Spirit Publishing Inc.
Minneapolis, MN
(612) 338-2068
help4kids@freespirit.com
www.freespirit.com

First published in 2013 by Franklin Watts, a division of Hachette Children's Books   ·   London, UK, and Sydney, Australia

Text © Franklin Watts 2013
Illustrations © Desideria Guicciardini 2013

The rights of Sue Graves to be identified as the author and Desideria Guicciardini as the illustrator of this Work have been asserted in accordance with the Copyright, Designs and Patents Act, 1988.

Editor: Jackie Hamley
Designer: Peter Scoulding